So Many Ways to
Build a Shelter

A new way to explore the animal kingdom

Editorial Director
Caroline Fortin

Research and Editing
Martine Podesto

Documentation
Anne-Marie Brault
Anne-Marie Labrecque

Cover Design
Épicentre

Page Setup
Lucie Mc Brearty

Illustrations
François Escalmel
Jocelyn Gardner

Translator
Gordon Martin

Copy Editing
Veronica Schami

D0503367

QUÉBEC AMÉRIQUE

A home of one's own

To hide from their predators, to protect themselves from bad weather or to care for their young, animals often build shelters. Some take refuge in cracks in rocks, at the tops of trees or in the undergrowth, while other more enterprising animals build very comfortable homes. Whether they dig into the ground, weave grasses together or cut wood, animals use all the tools they have at their disposal: their legs, their claws, their beaks, their muzzles and snouts, or their teeth. Building materials are abundant in nature: leaves, twigs, wood, earth, hair, down, wool, moss and even pieces of plastic and fabric. But some animals make their own building materials.

Saliva nests

To make their cup-shaped nests, swiftlets use a very original material: strands of their own saliva. During the mating season, these birds regurgitate long, thin, viscous filaments produced by the salivary glands under their tongue. The saliva hardens and rapidly sticks to the walls of the rocky caves the birds call home.

swiftlet
Collocalia fuciphaga

Are you curious?

Every year, men risk their lives to gather swiftlet nests, an Asian delicacy. In Hong Kong, a single bowl of swiftlet's nest soup can cost as much as $60!

An original house

Many small beetles have very special homes made entirely from excrement. As soon as the eggs are laid, the parents roll them in their excrement until they look like little dried fruits. Once the eggs hatch, the young creatures not only hang on to their coating, they enlarge it by adding their own excrement.

case-bearing leaf beetle
Clytra laeviuscula

Living in an air bubble

Spiders are famous for making webs. As its name suggests, the water spider lives underwater. It spins a small watertight globe of threads that it attaches to aquatic grasses. During its trips to the surface of the water, the spider traps small air bubbles in the hairs on its limbs. It then returns to its underwater home and fills it with the air bubbles. The spider is now perfectly safe in its chamber of air.

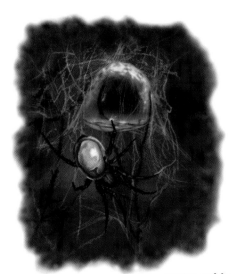

water spider
Argyroneta aquatica

A platform overlooking the sea

The lesser noddy, a sea bird, lives on the tropical islands of the Atlantic, Pacific and Indian Oceans. Its spacious home, which is often built on a rocky ledge, is made from its own feathers and excrement. Once they have been well mixed together and trampled on, these materials form a solid platform where the family can make itself at home.

lesser noddy
Anous tenuirostris

These ones move into prefabricated homes

Building a house takes a great deal of effort and energy. That's why it is often more convenient to look for a home that is already made to measure. Nature often provides natural shelters. A hollow tree trunk may be inhabited by owls, weasels, lemurs or parrots. A damp cave makes a very attractive home for bats, insects and birds – and even certain mammals such as bears – while cracks in rocks can house lizards, snakes, amphibians and insects. Some small animals greatly appreciate man-made structures. A crack in the wall of a house, a nesting box, the area underneath a cornice, a chimney – these are perfect places to set up the family home. Many animals also take refuge in structures built by other animals.

An owl among woodpeckers

This tiny 15-centimeter-long owl lives in the deserts of the southern United States. Active all night long and until the early morning, it is always hunting for food: grasshoppers, moths and beetles. At daylight, the elf owl settles comfortably into a hole drilled into a giant cactus by a woodpecker. Perfectly safe, it enjoys a well-deserved rest.

elf owl
Micrathene whitneyi

Are you curious?

The eyes of owls cannot move. To look in a different direction, these animals have to turn their whole head. Some species can turn their heads three quarters of the way around!

4

A bird trapped in a tree

Excrement, wet soil, rotten wood and saliva – that's the plaster recipe of the hornbill found in tropical forests. The female plugs up a natural hole in a tree trunk with this ingenious mixture. For two months, her mate slides small fruits and insects through a thin slit to feed mom and the kids. The snakes and monkeys that prey on hornbills neither see nor hear the young birds.

red-beaked hornbill
Tockus erythrorhynchus

Shelters in rock

Although many species of parrots make their nests in holes in trees, the bahamian amazon, a West Indian parrot, nests underground. The earth on the island of Abaco, its natural habitat, is made up of limestone in which water has already carved out deep cavities. The water has receded but the holes it created remain. They make perfect burrows for laying eggs and raising young amazons.

bahamian amazon
Amazona leucocephala bahamensis

5

How sly is the fox?

Foxes are found on almost every continent: North America, Europe, Africa, Asia and even Australia, where they were introduced by man. Although it sometimes digs its own dwelling, this beautiful mammal is quite happy to move into the burrows of other animals. It has a special fondness for badger burrows, which are found on sunny slopes.

red fox
Vulpes vulpes

These ones build underground shelters

In the wild, there are not enough natural burrows to accommodate all the animals that need homes. Most burrowing animals have to dig their own holes. The burrow of a hippopotamus is usually no more than an ordinary hole in the ground, shaped like a comfortable bathtub. A little deeper, the "craters" dug by female boars allow their offspring to rest in complete safety. Many animals bury themselves in the ground: cockles, sea urchins, sand fleas and snails, as well as the larvae of several insects. Underground burrows have many advantages. In addition to escaping their enemies on the surface, the animals find their underground refuges very convenient in bad weather.

A well-camouflaged home

The trap-door spider chooses very dry earth in which to dig its tube-shaped burrow with its hooks. Its cozy home, which is completely lined with silk, is kept secret by a little plug. Discreetly attached to the ground by a thread of silk, the cover of its home can be opened and closed at the whim of the spider. Insects should beware of getting too close: the cover will open and the spider will pounce.

trap-door spider
Theraphosidae family

Are you curious?

Trap-doors are very large spiders found mainly in tropical regions. Certain species attack very large prey. They have been seen capturing small birds, frogs, lizards and even snakes.

The phantom of the beaches

The phantom crab hollows out its U- or Y-shaped home in the sand of certain American beaches. It comes out of hiding at night to feed on debris and live prey left behind by the high tide, but spends the day at the very depths of its dwelling. The well-camouflaged entrance to its tunnel is blocked with sand.

ghost crab
Ocypode quadrata

Atlantic puffin
Fratercula arctica

Burrowing birds

The Atlantic puffins found in the cold seas of North America and Europe come ashore only to reproduce. These magnificent birds, which are closely related to auks, live in burrows they dig with their own beaks and claws. The thousands of couples that make up a single colony dig so many holes along the shoreline that the ground sometimes caves in.

7

A U-shaped hiding place

Where do those little twisted pieces of earth come from? The lugworm, a freshwater worm 20 centimeters long, lives completely camouflaged in the sand, where it digs its U-shaped hiding place. After making itself comfortable, the lugworm feeds on the tiny animals and plants in its sandy environment. Every 40 minutes or so, it deposits its digestive residue in strange little piles at the door of its home.

lugworm
Arenicola marina

These ones are
excellent potters

Earth is a very practical natural material. Readily available, it can be mixed with saliva, or even with excrement, to make dense mud. Animals that use earth as a building material construct very solid homes that are usually very long lasting because the mixture they use becomes as hard as plaster when it dries. Many birds, including owls, nuthatches and swifts, make little balls of clay that they stick together using their saliva as mortar. Insects such as wasps and bees also use dried mud to build homes of various shapes.

The heaviest nest

To construct its ball-shaped nest, the rufous hornero gathers 1,500 to 2,500 little piles of clay, then assembles them with grass, feathers and cow dung. These charming little mud houses, which are often found on branches or at the top of a post, take 10 to 15 days to build and can measure as much as 20 centimeters in diameter. And they can be used only once!

Are you curious?

The South American bird the rufous hornero is known as the "baker", because its round home looks like a little oven and becomes so hot within 20 to 26 days that the bird has no choice but to abandon it to avoid suffocation.

A pool of mud

Some tree frogs build mud shelters that look like small pools. In one South American species, the male constructs a circular pool about 30 centimeters in diameter, surrounded by a low wall 10 centimeters high. The couple deposits its eggs in the pool, where they are safe from predators unable to scale the wall of mud.

tree frog
Hyla faber

greater flamingo
Phoenicopterus ruber

A mud cone

The superb pink flamingos of Europe, Africa and the Middle East live in huge colonies. To make their nests, the males and females gather mud, stones, shells, feathers and grass. The nests are shaped, stamped on and slept on until the materials are well packed down. Cone-shaped, the nests can reach heights of 40 centimeters.

9

Potter wasps

To provide shelter for its offspring, the potter wasp constructs small urns from little balls of clay it makes after it rains. In each of these vases, the female lays a small egg that is suspended from the ceiling by a thread of silk. At the bottom of the urn, a caterpillar or a paralyzed insect waits to be devoured by the larva.

rufous hornero
Furnarius rufus

potter wasp
Eumenes pomiformis

These animals are master tunnel-builders

Some animals are not content to dig ordinary holes in the ground; they construct intricate networks of tunnels with birthing rooms, bedrooms, resting areas and toilets. These veritable underground buildings can house as many as several hundred individual animals and extend over a very large area. Some animals rarely have cause to leave their underground dwellings. They not only sleep in their shelters, they also build up a store of supplies, reproduce, raise their young and feed there. They thus have a cool, humid place to live all year long.

Veritable underground villages

The largest underground villages are those built by prairie dogs. Divided into several neighborhoods, the village is made up of hundreds of burrows, each of which is home to about 15 members of a single family. The complex structure of these burrows begins with a vertical corridor 3 to 4 meters long that leads to a series of tunnels culminating in various rooms. Perched on hillocks 30 centimeters high, which are made from the earth brought above ground, brave watchdogs stand guard at the entrance to the underground city. At the first sign of danger, they let out a characteristic yelp meaning: "Attention everyone, return to your homes right now!"

black-tailed prairie dogs
Cynomys ludovicianus

Are you curious?

Prairie dogs are not related to other dogs; they are actually hare-sized rodents found on the prairies of North America. They are referred to as dogs because their yelp sounds very much like a bark.

A house on two floors

The home of the pocket gopher has two stories: on the first, deeper level are little rooms and storage areas, while on the second are the bedroom and the long feeding corridors. This hamster-sized rodent is perfectly content with its role as a burrowing animal. Tireless, it continues to do excavation work even after it snows.

Eastern pocket gopher
Geomys bursarius

A place for everything

Cottontail rabbits, which live in colonies comprising approximately 100 individuals, dig branched burrows for shelter. However, when the female is ready to give birth, she digs a special hole known as a "nursery burrow" away from the rest of the colony. This hole, which is no more than 50 to 70 centimeters deep, is home to the baby rabbits.

Old World rabbit
Oryctolagus cuniculus

A temporary burrow

This strange animal with pointed ears, a pig's snout, a kangaroo's tail and a body covered with stiff hairs is known as the aardvark or "earth pig". A nomad of the African savannas, this mammal takes shelter from the intense heat in burrows it digs on its own as it makes its way across the grasslands. Small rodents, birds and snakes are more than happy to take up residence in these burrows once the aardvarks move on.

aardvark
Orycteropus afer

...and so are these

Animals that spend most of their time underground are perfectly adapted to this way of life. Since they live in the darkest possible environment, their eyes are of little use; that's why they are so small or, in some cases, nonexistent. Another important detail: since the flaps of ears can be a nuisance underground, they are either very small or completely absent in many of these species. To find their way around and search for food, burrowing animals rely on their senses of smell, hearing and touch. That's why these senses are particularly well-developed in these animals.

A champion burrower

The mole, a solitary animal, digs tunnels with its claws and shovel-like forelegs, while its rear legs push the earth to the surface. Little mounds formed by the excess earth, mole holes have an opening on the outside to let air in and out. Beneath the biggest mole hole is the main room, an area carpeted with leaves where moles rest after hunting.

12

European mole
Talpa europaea

A very clean burrow

This carnivorous mammal, which has short, powerful legs, is also a champion burrower. Its huge, 10-meter-long burrows, found on the steppes and prairies of the Americas, are remarkably clean. The parents' and children's rooms are carpeted with a layer of soft grass that the badger changes frequently. The tunnels can be up to five meters deep.

American badger
Taxidea taxus

Sheltered from the Australian sun

Like the koala and the kangaroo, the wombat is a marsupial. Using its teeth and claws, it digs its 15-meter-long burrow through clay soil that is as hard as rock. The wombat spends the entire day in its extremely comfortable refuge, where the temperature and humidity are just right. A good companion, the wombat is often content to share its shelter with snakes, lizards, birds and rabbits.

common wombat
Vombatus ursinus

Life in the dark

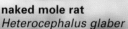

This odd-looking blind animal – with its pink, very wrinkled skin, short legs and flat head – will never win any beauty contests. It rarely leaves its underground dwelling, which is made up of long tunnels the mole rat digs with powerful incisors that remain outside of its mouth even when it is closed. Its impressive network of tunnels can cover an area as large as six football fields!

13

naked mole rat
Heterocephalus glaber

Are you curious?

Moles do some extraordinary things. Champion diggers, they can move 6 kilograms of earth in barely 20 minutes.

Others are
incredible artisans

Some animals are incredible artisans. Using their skillful beaks, agile limbs or teeth, they gather leaves, grass and silky threads to make finely crafted little homes. Birds are incredible weavers. Interlacing blades of grass with great skill, they knot, weave and braid to create real little marvels. The materials they use are long, flexible and sturdy: climbing plants, roots, ribbon-shaped leaves or even torn thin strips of broad leaves. The most extraordinary weaverbirds are found in Africa. These include whydahs, bishops, social weavers, queleas and certain species of chickadees.

Woven houses

Weaverbirds are aptly named: they are the best weavers in the animal kingdom. Their complex nest starts out as just a simple ring of interwoven grass; the male bird then adds and weaves in plant materials of his choice. There are approximately 70 species of weaverbirds in Africa and Asia. Although all their nests look like little purses dangling from trees, the appearance of the birds varies from species to species.

14

masked weaver
Ploceus heuglini

Are you
curious?

Among weaverbirds, nest building is a means of seduction. The female inspects the work done by the male, then shows her appreciation. If she likes the nest, she accepts the male as her companion.

A quick builder

It takes the small harvest mouse only 5 to 10 hours to construct its pretty woven nest. A ball of dried grass, the nest is perched almost one meter above the ground on a long stalk of wheat or stem of grass. Using its teeth and legs, the rodent tears the grass into thin strips, which it then weaves into a ball. The inside of the nest is carpeted with leaves and moss.

Old World harvest mouse
Micromys minutus

A big designer

The Asian tailorbird builds its nest from broad leaves and spider silk. It does this by folding two leaves together or rolling one into the shape of a cone. Using its beak as a needle, it then pierces little holes along the edges of the leaves and sews them together with the spider silk. The inside of the leaf is carpeted with a soft, warm layer of plants, sheep's wool and animal hair.

long-tailed tailor-bird
Orthotomus sutorius

Designing larvae

The weaver ants of Asian jungles work in teams to construct their pretty houses. While several ants hold the leaves in place, others walk young larvae across the joined leaves. These larvae produce threads of silk in glands located just below their mouths. The thousands of threads of silk are arranged in a way that provides solid support for the walls of the dwelling.

weaver ants
Oecophylla longinoda

These ones are master drillers

Whether they are digging holes in the ground, shaping earth or weaving and knotting twigs, animals that build their own shelters do work that requires time, energy, strength and skill. Just hollowing out earth to make a burrow must be extraordinarily difficult and tiring. But some animals accomplish tasks that require incredible strength: they are known as borers. They carve out homes in extremely hard substances such as wood and even rock. It seems unbelievable that very small animals can expend so much energy building a home. Yet the beaks and powerful jaws of certain animals manage to do work that humans would never be able to do with their bare hands.

Cliffs like rounds of Swiss cheese

Each of the 24 species of bee-eaters chooses the ideal location to hollow out its home: a sandy riverbank, the sunny slope of a hill, a rock face or the roof of an animal's lair. Hovering next to the chosen location, the bird makes an opening with its pointed, sturdy beak and continues to dig without respite for days on end. At the end of the tunnel, there is a small down-covered room for the young birds.

carmine bee-eater
Merops nubicus

16

Are you curious?

The bee-eaters found in the hot regions of Europe, Africa, Asia, Australia and the Philippines are not the only birds that live in burrows; so do kingfishers and bank swallows.

Tunneling through wood

The female goat-moth, or willow borer, lays hundreds of eggs in the cracked bark of several kinds of leafy trees. Fourteen days later, small caterpillars with powerful jaws emerge from the eggs. For over two years, they dig tunnels in the wood of the tree, where they will be well protected from their enemies. These extraordinary networks of tunnels can sometimes block the sap and kill the tree.

goat-moth caterpillar
Cossus cossus

common piddock
Pholas dactylus

The perseverance of a mollusk

At birth, the tiny larva of the piddock attaches itself to a limestone rock. The shell, which emerges gradually, has small, pointed, sawtooth-like structures on one end. Patiently and methodically, the mollusk, which is about the size of a mussel, pivots until it has bored a deep hole in the rock, where it can hide from prying eyes.

17

A houseproud homebody

Some woodpeckers peck their homes in earth, cactuses or ant-hills. Others, who are used to cutting wood in order to feed, do not have any trouble hollowing out nests in tree trunks. These dwellings are often big enough to accommodate owls and squirrels. Black woodpeckers can occupy the same home for 4 to 6 years, unless it is stolen by another animal.

black woodpecker
Dryocopus martius

These ones are
talented architects

Who are the giants responsible for building such impressive dwellings? These extraordinarily large structures are the work of animals who are no bigger than most of their fellow creatures. More often than not, the key to their success is patience: some of them devote several months of every year to building a shelter. But that's not their only secret. Animals that live in colonies sometimes band together to construct their home. The dwellings of these entrepreneurial animals often last for quite some time, even for several years.

A majestic nest

The golden eagle builds its gigantic nest at the top of a tree or on the steep face of a cliff. Constructed with branches up to two meters long, this extraordinary structure can be up to four and a half meters wide and can weigh more than two tons! The energy expended to construct this enormous shelter is not wasted because the golden eagle, which can live for as long as 46 years, occupies the same nest throughout its life.

golden eagle
Aquila chrysaetos

Are you curious?

There are over 30 species of eagles, and they inhabit all parts of the world except New Zealand and Antarctica. The most common species, the golden eagle, is found in Europe, Asia and North America. It has a wingspan of two and a half meters.

18

Strength in numbers

Many of the 9,500 species of ants in existence construct ant-hills in the form of mounds, but the hill of the wood ant is the most impressive. Built on top of an old stump, it is made up of earth, conifer needles and dry twigs. Under the two-meter-high mound are several tunnels comprising the winter quarters. The dwelling can provide shelter for up to a million ants.

wood ant
Formica rufa

social weaver
Philetairus socius

A collective nest

Social weaverbirds live in colonies of about 100 couples. Together, they build the largest collective nests in existence. Under the large common roof, each small family has its own individual dwelling with an opening at the bottom. Made from grass and branches, the nests of social weavers can be up to five meters in diameter. Some of these structures have been inhabited for over 100 years.

19

A megaproject

To construct its nest, this bird, which is about the size of a small chicken, works for 11 months a year, from morning till night. Using its large feet, it digs a hole one meter deep, then fills it with damp leaves and branches, which it covers with a mound of sand one meter high. As it rots, the plant material releases the heat required for the incubation of the eggs.

mallee fowl
Leipoa ocellata

...as are these
ones

Humans have definitely looked to animals for inspiration. Animals were the first great engineers and architects on Earth. Obeying complex laws of physics and mathematics, many animals have created veritable natural masterpieces. The ingenuity of animals never ceases to amaze. In animal societies, where each individual plays a crucial role, nothing is left to chance.

Monumental dwellings

Living in highly organized colonies, certain termites construct fabulous dwellings that are extraordinarily large. These termitariums have thick walls and are made from a mixture of earth or wood, excrement and saliva that becomes as hard as cement when baked in the sun. The structure is made up of a royal chamber, compartments for the eggs and a food-storage area. It is ventilated by a network of interior chimneys.

Are you curious?

People sometimes salvage the earth from abandoned termitariums to make bricks for building houses. A single termitarium in Africa is said to have provided 4,500 of these bricks!

termite
Isoptera order

Cardboard houses

Wasps have been making and using paper for a very long time. Their pretty hanging cardboard dwellings can shelter up to 200 individuals. To produce their building material, wasps pull small pieces of wood from trees, houses or fences, then mix them with their saliva by chewing. This creates a fine pulp that turns into stiff paper as it dries.

paper wasp
Polistinae subfamily

Wax rooms

Worker bees often choose to construct their wax dwellings in a hollow tree. Secreted by three tiny holes located below their abdomen, the wax is used to build a hive. Each small chamber or "cell" of the hive is a hexagon whose symmetry is monitored by the extremely sensitive antennae and legs of the bees. The cells are used to store the honey and the pollen, or to receive the eggs.

honeybee
Apis mellifera

A champion builder

Using its powerful jaws and sharp incisors, the tireless beaver chops down, strips and transports tree trunks and branches to build its dam and lodge. By keeping the water level constant, the dam allows the beaver to swim, find food and build its lodge throughout the year. Made from branches, stones and mud, the lodge has discreet underwater entrances and, just above the level of the water, a cozy room for the beaver's family.

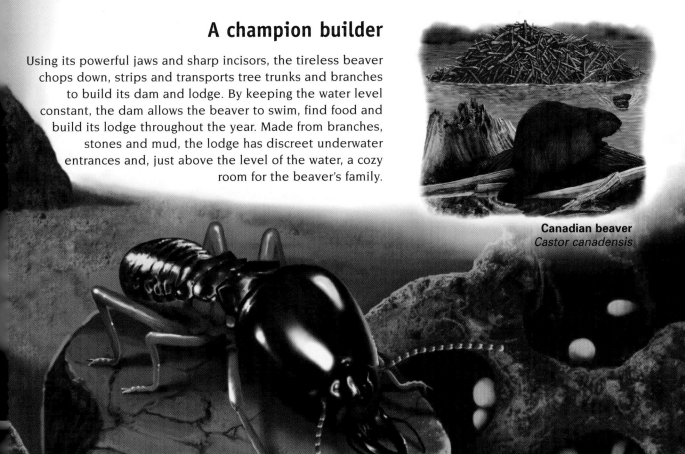

Canadian beaver
Castor canadensis

These ones have temporary homes

Some animals need shelter for only a few hours a day – during sleep, for example, when they are most vulnerable. These animals often take refuge in special little dwellings. Others have a life cycle with several different stages: insects that become magnificent butterflies must first survive as eggs, larvae and chrysalises. Some of these life-forms are particularly fragile! During their metamorphosis, many insects make themselves a cocoon in which they take shelter from their potentially fatal environment.

The comfort of silk

The caterpillar turns into a butterfly during a phenomenon known as "pupation". This is a very delicate stage in the life of the animal. Several species of caterpillars go through this transformation inside a cocoon of silk they make themselves. The silk, produced by two special glands located at the level of their lower lip, is secreted as a liquid and becomes solid in the presence of the oxygen in air.

silkworm
Bombyx mori

Are you curious?

In Asia, silkworms are raised by the millions. Each silkworm cocoon contains hundreds of meters of silk thread. These threads are reprocessed and used to make magnificent fabrics.

A cover for the night

Many of the parrotfish found in tropical seas wrap themselves in a cozy cover for the night. Their cocoon, which is made from mucous secreted by their skin glands, is open at the front and back to allow water to flow through it freely. This allows the fish to breathe easily. It takes the parrotfish 30 minutes to make its shelter and another 30 to dispose of it.

parrotfish
Scarus vetula

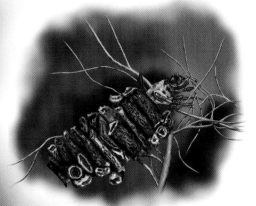

caddis fly
Trichoptera order

A fleeting existence

As soon as it is born, the larva of the caddis fly builds its shelter from various materials such as the tips of plants, fragments of shells, pieces of seaweed and sand. Underwater, it captures and cuts up its building materials, then glues them together with the silk it secretes. Perfectly camouflaged inside its tube, it patiently awaits its transformation. Caddis flies, which look like little gray butterflies, live for only the few hours required to mate.

A house in the trees

Some large apes make comfortable beds where they can spend the night with their family. Every night, the female gorilla of the African forests constructs a platform of interlacing branches on which she places a small bed of soft leaves, just large enough for her and her child. The male builds his own bed, but he soon outgrows his treetop shelter and has to abandon it to sleep on the ground.

gorilla
Gorilla gorilla

...while these ones have
no shelter at all

Not all animals are skilled builders and their environment does not always provide them with building materials. Some animals have no choice but to spend their nights under the stars and their days in the full light of the sun.

A makeshift nest

Emperor penguins live in Antarctica, on ice that is permanently frozen. After laying their eggs, the females return to the sea, leaving the males to protect the precious embryos for the entire winter. Huddled closely together, the males prevent the eggs from touching the ice by keeping them on top of their feet, which serve as a sort of nest.

common murre
Uria aalge

Are you curious?

Although they resemble the auks found in the Northern hemisphere, penguins are not related to them in any way. Unlike auks, penguins cannot fly; their wings are very much like large fins.

Dozing in a bed of seaweed

This charming little marine mammal, which inhabits cold seas, certainly cannot build a shelter in the watery depths: like all mammals, it needs air to survive. So how does it get any rest? When night falls, it lies on its back and wraps its body in a pile of seaweed, which supports it and prevents it from floating away. There, not far from shore, the sea otter can rest undisturbed.

sea otter
Enhydra lutris

A safe place to rest

Deer have no fixed address. To rest, they choose a comfortable location where they are shielded from danger. Active at night, deer often gather in a clearing during the day. When in a group, the animals feel secure. If the location is peaceful, they will return to it. The scent of the animals becomes so strong in these clearings that it can even be detected by humans.

25

red deer
Cervus elaphus

giant panda
Ailuropoda melanoleuca

No need for shelter

The giant panda found in bamboo forests does not have to build a shelter. Its thick, oil-rich fur protects it from the dampness and the cold of the Chinese and Tibetan forests. To rest, the panda leans against a rock or a tree, or rolls itself into a ball on the ground. Placing its head on a soft carpet of conifer needles, it sleeps peacefully.

1. **Swiflet (p. 2)**
   (Southeast Asia)

2. **Case-bearing leaf beetle (p. 3)**
   (almost all of France)

3. **Water spider (p. 3)**
   (almost all of France, much of Europe)

4. **Lesser noddy (p. 3)**
   (Pacific islands and tropical Atlantic islands)

5. **Elf owl (p. 4)**
   (southwestern United States, eastern Central America)

6. **Red-beaked hornbill (p. 5)**
   (western, central and eastern Africa, south of the Sahara)

7. **Bahamian amazon (p. 5)**
   (Bahamas)

8. **Red fox (p. 5)**
   (Northern hemisphere, from the Arctic Circle to North Africa and from the deserts of Central America to the Asian steppes)

9. **Trap-door spider (p. 6)**
   (South America, Central America, Mexico, Arizona, Africa, Australia, Malaysia and Southeast Asia)

10. **Ghost crab (p. 7)**
    (from Rhode Island to Santa Catarina in Brazil)

11. **Atlantic puffin (p. 7)**
    (North Atlantic)

12. **Lugworm (p. 7)**
    (coastal areas of Europe)

13. **Rufous hornero (p. 9)**
    (temperate and subtropical areas of South America)

14. **Tree frog (p. 9)**
    (Brazil and Argentina)

15. **Greater flamingo (p. 9)**
    (Caribbean, from southern Europe to South Africa)

16. **Potter wasp (p. 9)**
    (Europe, much of Asia, North Africa and North America)

17. **Black-tailed prairie dog (p. 10)**
    (United States and extreme north of Mexico)

18. **Eastern pocket gopher (p. 11)**
    (North America, from the Canadian border to Mexico)

19. **Old world rabbit (p. 11)**
    (Europe, northwestern Africa, introduced into numerous countries including Australia, New Zealand and Chile)

20. **Aardvark (p. 11)**
    (Africa, south of the Sahara)

21. **European mole (p. 12)**
    (Europe, Asia)

22. **American badger (p. 13)**
    (from southwestern Canada to central Mexico)

23. **Common wombat (p. 13)**
    (southeastern Australia and Tasmania)

24. **Naked mole rat (p. 13)**
    (eastern Africa: Ethiopia, Somalia and Kenya)

MATERIALS FOR ALL TASTES		
	Animal	**Materials**
Insects	Paper wasp (Polistinae subfamily)	Wood fibers and saliva
	Goat-moth caterpillar (Trichoptera order)	Small pieces of wood, twigs, sand, gravel, snail shells
	Weaver ants (*Oecophylla longinoda*)	Fresh leaves and silk
Fish	Threespine stickleback (*Gasterosteus aculeatus*)	Plant debris and glutinous secretions
Birds	Woodcock (*Scolopax rusticola*)	Dead leaves
	Bowerbirds (Ptilonorhynchidae family)	Twigs, moss, snail shells, berries, insects, flowers, leaves, mushrooms, pieces of charcoal
	Swiftlet (*Collocalia* genus)	Saliva
	Rufous hornero (Furnariidae family)	Earth
	Calliope hummingbird (*Stellula calliope*)	Spider's web, lichen, moss, plants
Amphibians and reptiles	African tree frog (Rhacophoridae family)	Foam produced from a viscous liquid secreted by the frog
	Morelet's crocodile (*Crocodylus moreletii*)	Mud, branches and rotting leaves
Mammals	Beaver (*Castor fiber*)	Wood, mud, stones
	Muskrat (*Ondatra zibethicus*)	Reed mace and mud
	Squirrel (Sciuridae family)	Dead leaves, twigs, moss, sod bark, lichen, feathers, wool
	Opossum (Didelphidae family)	Leaves and grasses
	Gorilla (*Gorilla gorilla*)	Leaves

NEST-BUILDING BIRDS AND THEIR RECORDS

Bird	Dimensions of nest	Record
Calliope hummingbird *Stellula calliope*	Diameter: 2 cm Height: 3 cm	The smallest nest
Ostrich *Struthio camelus*	Diameter: 3 m	The nest that contains the biggest eggs
Golden eagle *Aquila chrysaetos*	Height: 2 m Diameter: 3 m	The largest elevated nest
Social weaver *Philetairus socius*	Diameter: 5 m	The largest collective nest
Common scrubfowl *Megapodius freycinet*	Diameter: 12 m Height: 5 m	The largest nest on the ground

A HOME OF ONE'S OWN

	Animal	Dwelling
Wild animals	Wasp	Wasp nest
	Termite	Termitarium
	Ant	Anthill
	Bee	Hive
	Mole	Burrow
	Bird	Nest
	Rabbit	Burrow
	Hare	Form
	Fox	Den
	Beaver	Lodge
	Boar	Wallow
	Snake	Lair
	Tiger	Den
	Wolf	Den
	Bear	Den
	Bat	Cave
	Mouse	Hole
Farm animals	Horse	Stable
	Cow	Shed
	Hen	Henhouse
	Pig	Hog house
	Sheep	Sheepfold
	Dog	Kennel

swiftlet
Collocalia fuciphaga

class	Aves
order	Apodiformes
family	Apodidae

distribution	Southeast Asia
habitat	limestone caves of tropical forests
diet	spiders, insects
reproduction	1 or 2 eggs per clutch
predators	birds of prey, nests eaten by humans

elf owl
Micrathene whitneyi

class	Aves
order	Strigiformes
family	Strigidae

distribution	southwestern United States, eastern Central America
habitat	arid regions with giant cacti
diet	grasshoppers, beetles, moths, caterpillars
reproduction	3 to 5 eggs per clutch
predators	no specific predators

trap-door spider

class	Arachnida
order	Araneida
family	Theraphosidae

size	2.5 to 11 cm
distribution	America: Mexico, Arizona; Africa, Australia, Malaysia, Southeast Asia
habitat	terrestrial or arboreal
diet	insects, lizards
reproduction	500 to 1,000 eggs per summer
predators	native people, wasps, mammals, birds, amphibians
life span	up to 25 years

rufous hornero
Furnarius rufus

class	Aves
order	Passeriformes
family	Furnariidae

size and weight	approximately 19 cm, 75 g
distribution	temperate and subtropical regions of South America
habitat	wooded prairies
diet	soil insects, spiders, worms, mollusks
reproduction	3 or 4 eggs per clutch
predators	buzzards

black-tailed prairie dog
Cynomys ludovicianus

class	Mammalia
order	Rodentia
family	Sciuridae

size and weight	37.5 cm including the tail, 0.7 to 1.4 kg
distribution	United States and extreme north of Mexico
habitat	dry western prairies
diet	mainly vegetarian
reproduction	2 to 10 young per litter
predators	birds of prey
life span	up to 9 years

European mole
Talpa europaea

class	Mammalia
order	Insectivora
family	Talpidae

size and weight	13 to 20 cm including the tail, 60 to 120 g
distribution	Europe, Asia
habitat	ground of woods and fields
diet	arthropods and worms
reproduction	3 to 4 young per litter
predators	owls, herons, weasels, ermines, badgers, foxes, cats
life span	3 years

masked weaver
Ploceus heuglini

class	Aves
order	Passeriformes
family	Ploceidae

size	14 cm
distribution	Senegal, northwestern Kenya
habitat	semiarid and wooded savannas
diet	grasses, insects
reproduction	2 or 3 eggs, sometimes 2 clutches

carmine bee-eater
Merops nubicus

class	Aves
order	Coraciiformes
family	Meropidae

size	28 cm including the tail
distribution	western, central and southern Africa
habitat	prairies with scattered trees
diet	grasshoppers, ants, wasps, other insects
reproduction	3 to 5 eggs per clutch
predators	birds of prey, lizards, snakes, man
life span	up to 7 years

golden eagle
Aquila chrysaetos

class	Aves
order	Falconiformes
family	Accipitridae

size and weight	75 to 88 cm, 2.8 to 6.6 kg
distribution	Eurasia, North America, North Africa
habitat	taiga, massifs
diet	small mammals, birds, reptiles, carrion
reproduction	1 to 2 eggs per year
life span	25 years in the wild

termite

class	Insecta
order	Isoptera
family	there are 7 families of termites

size	15 to 22 mm
distribution	North America, Asia, Europe, Australia, Africa, South America
habitat	forests
diet	wood, plant debris, mushrooms
predators	aardvarks, pangolins, anteaters, armadillos, birds, aardwolves
reproduction	1 egg every 2 seconds, for 15 years or more

silkworm
Bombyx mori

class	Insecta
order	Lepidoptera
family	Bombycidae

size	5-cm wingspan
distribution	native to China; cultivated in India, Japan, Spain, France, Italy
habitat	artificial breeding environment
diet	blackberry leaves for the caterpillars; the adults do not feed
reproduction	300 to 400 eggs in breeding conditions
predators	insectivores
life span	60 days

common murre
Uria aalge

class	Aves
order	Charadriiformes
family	Alcidae

size and weight	40 cm long, 1 kg
distribution	northern Atlantic and Pacific coasts of North America, northern Europe, Greenland, Iceland
habitat	coastal waters; nest in cliffs
diet	fish, crustaceans, mollusks, worms
reproduction	just 1 egg
predators	no specific predators

Glossary

Amphibian

An animal, such as the frog, that can live on land or in water.

Aquatic

Growing or living in or near water.

Artisan

A worker who practises a trade or handicraft.

Beetle

An insect whose rear wings are protected, when at rest, by a second, harder pair.

Borer

Any of various insects, insect larvae, mollusks or crustaceans that bore into hard material.

Branched

Divided into several branches or sections.

Burrower

Any animal that digs or tunnels through the ground.

Chrysalis

The intermediate stage in the life cycle of lepidoptera, between the caterpillar and the butterfly.

Colony

A group of animals that live together as part of a community.

Digger

A worker that digs, turns over or moves earth to change the shape of a site.

Filament

Any organic structure or part shaped like a long thin thread.

Gallery

An underground tunnel or passageway dug by a burrowing animal.

Gland

An organ that produces a secretion, a relatively thick liquid.

Globe

Any sphere-shaped covering.

Hexagonal

Having six angles and six sides.

Incubation

The act of sitting on an egg to provide the heat required for the development of the embryo.

Limestone

A sedimentary rock consisting mainly of calcium carbonate.

Mammal

Any animal species in which the female has mammary glands for feeding her young.

Mane

The long coarse hair that grows from the neck of certain animals, especially horses.

Marsupial

Any animal species in which the female has a ventral pouch containing mammary glands for carrying and feeding her young after birth.

Metamorphosis

A complete change in form or state that occurs among certain animals; the caterpillar undergoes a radical transformation of this kind when it becomes a butterfly.

Mortar

A mixture of various substances builders use to bond or cover materials.

Mucus

A transparent viscous liquid.

Offspring

All of the children or young of a human or animal.

Predator

An animal that feeds on prey.

Pulp

A soggy and malleable paste-like substance.

Secrete

To produce and release a substance.

Slope

A side or an incline of a mountain.

Snout

The muzzle of a boar or pig.

Stationary

Remaining in one place for a certain amount of time.

Steppe

An extensive grassy plain with no trees, a dry climate and little vegetation.

Structure

The manner in which the parts of a whole are arranged and how they are interrelated.

Tropical

Located in the regions between the tropics of Cancer and Capricorn, where it never gets cold.

Twist

Something twisted or rolled back on itself.

Vegetation

The plant life of a particular region.

Wingspan

The distance between the tips of fully spread wings.

Index

The terms in **bold characters** refer to an illustration; those in *italics* indicate a keyword.

So Many Ways to Build a Shelter was created and produced by **QA International**, a division of
Les Éditions Québec Amérique inc. 329, rue de la Commune Ouest, 3ᵉ étage, Montréal (Québec) H2Y 2E1 Canada **T** 514.499.3000 **F** 514.499.3010
©1998 Éditions Québec Amérique inc.

ISBN 2-89037-960-4

Printed and bound in Canada

10 9 8 7 6 5 4 3 2 1   99 98